Dreams

By

Jerome K. Jerome

British Library Cataloguing-in-Publication Data
A catalogue record for this book is available from the
British Library

Jerome K. Jerome

Jerome Klapka Jerome was born in Walsall, England in 1859. Both his parents died while he was in his early teens, and he was forced to quit school to support himself. Jerome worked for a number of years collecting coal along railway tracks, before trying his hand at acting, journalism, teaching and soliciting. At long last, in 1885, he had some success with *On the Stage – and Off*, a comic memoir of his experiences with an acting troupe. Jerome produced a number of essays over the following years, and married in 1888, spending the honeymoon in "a little boat" on the Thames.

In 1889, Jerome published his most successful and best-remembered work, *Three Men in a Boat*. Featuring himself and two of his friends encountering humorous situations while floating down the Thames in a small boat, the book was an instant success, and has never been out of print. In fact, its popularity was such that the number of registered Thames boats went up fifty percent in the year following its publication. With the financial security provided by *Three Men in a Boat*, Jerome was able to dedicate himself fully to writing, producing eleven more novels and a number of anthologies of short fiction.

In 1926, Jerome published his autobiography, *My Life and Times*. He died a year later, aged 68.

The most extraordinary dream I ever had was one in which I fancied that, as I was going into a theater, the cloak-room attendant stopped me in the lobby and insisted on my leaving my legs behind me.

I was not surprised; indeed, my acquaintanceship with theater harpies would prevent my feeling any surprise at such a demand, even in my waking moments; but I was, I must honestly confess, considerably annoyed. It was not the payment of the cloak-room fee that I so much minded—I offered to give that to the man then and there. It was the parting with my legs that I objected to.

I said I had never heard of such a rule being attempted to be put in force at any respectable theater before, and that I considered it a most absurd and vexatious regulation. I also said I should write to The Times about it.

The man replied that he was very sorry, but that those were his instructions. People complained that they could not get to and from their seats comfortably, because other people's legs were always in the way; and it had, therefore, been decided that, in future, everybody should leave their legs outside.

It seemed to me that the management, in making this order, had clearly gone beyond their legal right; and, under ordinary circumstances, I should have disputed it.

Being present, however, more in the character of a guest than in that of a patron, I hardly like to make a disturbance; and so I sat down and meekly prepared to comply with the demand.

I had never before known that the human leg did unscrew. I had always thought it was a fixture. But the man showed me how to undo them, and I found that they came off quite easily.

The discovery did not surprise me any more than the original request that I should take them off had done. Nothing does surprise one in a dream.

I dreamed once that I was going to be hanged; but I was not at all surprised about it. Nobody was. My relations came to see me off, I thought, and to wish me "Good-by!" They all came, and were all very pleasant; but they were not in the least astonished—not one of them. Everybody appeared to regard the coming tragedy as one of the most-naturally-to-be-expected things in the world.

They bore the calamity, besides, with an amount of stoicism that would have done credit to a Spartan father. There was no fuss, no scene. On the contrary, an atmosphere of mild cheerfulness prevailed.

Yet they were very kind. Somebody—an uncle, I think—left me a packet of sandwiches and a little something in a flask, in case, as he said, I should feel peckish on the scaffold.

It is "those twin-jailers of the daring" thought, Knowledge and Experience, that teach us surprise. We are surprised and incredulous when, in novels and plays, we come across good men and women, because Knowledge and Experience have taught us how rare and problematical is the existence of such people. In waking life, my friends and relations would, of course, have been surprised at hearing that I had committed a murder, and was, in consequence, about to be hanged, because Knowledge and Experience would have taught them that, in a country where the law is powerful and the police alert, the Christian citizen is usually pretty successful in withstanding the voice of temptation, prompting him to commit crime of an illegal character.

But into Dreamland, Knowledge and Experience do not enter. They stay without, together with the dull, dead clay of which they form a part; while the freed brain, released from their narrowing tutelage, steals softly past the ebon gate, to wanton at its own sweet will among the mazy paths that wind through the garden of Persephone.

Nothing that it meets with in that eternal land astonishes it because, unfettered by the dense conviction of our waking mind, that nought outside the ken of our own vision can in this universe be, all things to it are possible and even probable. In dreams, we fly and wonder not—except that we never flew before. We go naked, yet are not ashamed, though we mildly wonder what the police are about that they do not stop us. We converse with our dead, and think it was unkind that they did not come back to us before. In dreams, there happens that which human language cannot tell. In dreams, we see "the light that never was on sea or land," we hear the sounds that never yet were heard by waking ears.

It is only in sleep that true imagination ever stirs within us. Awake, we never imagine anything; we merely alter, vary, or transpose. We give another twist to the kaleidoscope of the things we see around us, and obtain another pattern; but not one of us has ever added one tiniest piece of new glass to the toy.

A Dean Swift sees one race of people smaller, and another race of people larger than the race of people that live down his own streets. And he also sees a land where the horses take the place of men. A Bulwer Lytton lays the scene of one of his novels inside the earth instead of outside. A Rider Haggard introduces us to a lady whose age is a few years more than the average woman would care to confess to; and pictures crabs larger than the usual shilling or eighteen-penny size. The number of so called imaginative writers who visit the moon is legion, and for all the novelty that they find, when they get there, they might just as well have gone to Putney. Others are continually drawing for us visions of the world one hundred or one thousand years hence. There is always a depressing absence of human nature about the place; so much so, that one feels great consolation in the thought, while reading, that we ourselves shall be comfortably dead and buried before the picture can be realized. In these prophesied Utopias everybody is painfully good and clean and happy, and all the work is done by electricity.

There is somewhat too much electricity, for my taste, in these worlds to come. One is reminded of those pictorial enamel-paint advertisements that one sees about so often now, in which all the members of an extensive household are represented as gathered together in one room, spreading enamel-paint over everything they can lay their hands upon. The old man is on a step-ladder, daubing the walls and ceiling with "cuckoo's-egg green," while the parlor-maid and the cook are on their knees, painting the floor with "sealing-wax red." The old lady is doing the picture frames in "terra cotta." The eldest daughter and her young man are making sly love in a corner over a pot of "high art yellow," with which, so soon as they have finished wasting their time, they will, it is manifest, proceed to elevate the piano. Younger brothers and sisters are busy freshening up the chairs and tables with "strawberry-jam pink" and "jubilee magenta." Every blessed thing in that room is being coated with enamel paint, from the sofa to the fire-irons, from the sideboard to the eight-day clock. If there is any paint left over, it will be used up for the family Bible and the canary.

It is claimed for this invention that a little child can make as much mess with it as can a grown-up person, and so all the children of the family are represented in the picture as hard at work, enameling whatever few articles of furniture and household use the grasping selfishness of their elders has spared to them. One is painting the toasting fork in a "skim-milk blue," while another is giving aesthetical value to the Dutch oven by means of a new shade of art green. The bootjack is being renovated in "old gold," and the baby is sitting on the floor, smothering its own cradle with "flush-upon-a-maiden's cheek peach color."

One feels that the thing is being overdone. That family, before another month is gone, will be among the strongest opponents of enamel paint that the century has produced. Enamel paint will be the ruin of that once happy home. Enamel paint has a cold, glassy, cynical appearance. Its presence everywhere about the place will begin to irritate the old man in the course of a week or so. He will call it, "This damn'd sticky stuff!" and will tell the wife that he wonders she didn't paint herself and the children with it while she was about it. She will reply, in an exasperatingly quiet tone of voice, that she does like that. Perhaps he will say next, that she did not warn him against it, and tell him what an idiot he was making of himself, spoiling the whole house with his foolish fads. Each one will persist that it was the other one who first suggested the absurdity, and they will sit up in bed and quarrel about it every night for a month.

The children having acquired a taste for smudging the concoction about, and there being nothing else left untouched in the house, will try to enamel the cat; and then there will be bloodshed, and broken windows, and spoiled infants, and sorrows and yells. The smell of the paint will make everybody ill; and the servants will give notice. Tradesmen's boys will lean up against places that are not dry and get their clothes enameled and claim compensation. And the baby will suck the paint off its cradle and have fits.

But the person that will suffer most will, of course, be the eldest daughter's young man. The eldest daughter's young man is always unfortunate. He means well, and he tries hard. His great ambition is to make the family love him. But fate is ever against him, and he only succeeds in gaining their undisguised contempt. The fact of his being "gone" on their Emily is, of itself, naturally sufficient to stamp him as an imbecile in the eyes of Emily's brothers and sisters. The father finds him slow, and thinks the girl might have done better; while the best that his future mother-in-law (his sole supporter) can say for him is, that he seems steady.

There is only one thing that prompts the family to tolerate him, and that is the reflection that he is going to take Emily away from them.

On that understanding they put up with him.

The eldest daughter's young man, in this particular case, will, you may depend upon it, choose that exact moment when the baby's life is hovering in the balance, and the cook is waiting for her wages with her box in the hall, and a coal-heaver is at the front door with a policeman, making a row about the damage to his trousers, to come in, smiling, with a specimen pot of some new high art, squashed-tomato-shade enamel paint, and suggest that they should try it on the old man's pipe.

Then Emily will go off into hysterics, and Emily's male progenitor will firmly but quietly lead that ill-starred yet true-hearted young man to the public side of the garden-gate; and the engagement will be "off."

Too much of anything is a mistake, as the man said when his wife presented him with four new healthy children in one day. We should practice moderation in all matters. A little enamel paint would have been good. They might have enameled the house inside and out, and have left the furniture alone. Or they might have colored the furniture, and let the house be. But an entirely and completely enameled home—a home, such as enamel-paint manufacturers love to picture on their advertisements, over which the yearning eye wanders in vain, seeking one single square inch of un-enameled matter—is, I am convinced, a mistake. It may be a home that, as the testimonials assure us, will easily wash. It may be an "artistic" home; but the average man is not yet educated up to the appreciation of it. The average man does not care for high art. At a certain point, the average man gets sick of high art.

So, in these coming Utopias, in which out unhappy grandchildren will have to drag out their colorless existence, there will be too much electricity. They will grow to loathe electricity.

Electricity is going to light them, warm them, carry them, doctor them, cook for them, execute them, if necessary. They are going to be weaned on electricity, rocked in their cradles by electricity, slapped by electricity, ruled and regulated and guided by electricity, buried by electricity. I may be wrong, but I rather think they are going to be hatched by electricity.

In the new world of our progressionist teachers, it is electricity that is the real motive-power. The men and women are only marionettes—worked by electricity.

But it was not to speak of the electricity in them, but of the originality in them, that I referred to these works of fiction. There is no originality in them whatever. Human thought is incapable of originality. No man ever yet imagined a new thing—only some variation or extension of an old thing.

The sailor, when he was asked what he would do with a fortune, promptly replied:

"Buy all the rum and 'baccy there is in the world."

"And what after that?" they asked him.

"Eh?"

"What would you buy after that—after you had bought up all the rum and tobacco there was in the world—what would you buy then?"

"After that? Oh! 'um!" (a long pause). "Oh!" (with inspiration) "why, more 'baccy!"

Rum and tobacco he knew something of, and could therefore imagine about. He did not know any other luxuries, therefore he could not conceive of any others.

So if you ask one of these Utopian-dreaming gentry what, after they had secured for their world all the electricity there was in the Universe, and after every mortal thing in their ideal Paradise, was done and said and thought by electricity, they could imagine as further necessary to human happiness, they would probably muse for awhile, and then reply, "More electricity."

They know electricity. They have seen the electric light, and heard of electric boats and omnibuses. They have possibly had an electric shock at a railway station for a penny.

Therefore, knowing that electricity does three things, they can go on and "imagine" electricity doing three hundred things, and the very great ones among them can imagine it doing three thousand things; but for them, or anybody else, to imagine a new force, totally unconnected with and different from anything yet known in nature, would be utterly impossible.

Human thought is not a firework, ever shooting off fresh forms and shapes as it burns; it is a tree, growing very slowly—you can watch it long and see no movement—very silently, unnoticed. It was planted in the world many thousand years ago, a tiny, sickly plant. And men guarded it and tended it, and gave up life and fame to aid its growth. In the hot days of their youth, they came to the gate of the garden and knocked, begging to be let in, and to be counted among the gardeners. And their young companions without called to them to come back, and play the man with bow and spear, and win sweet smiles from rosy lips, and take their part amid the feast, and dance, not stoop with wrinkled brows, at weaklings' work. And the passers by mocked them and called shame, and others cried out to stone them. And still they stayed there laboring, that the tree might grow a little, and they died and were forgotten.

And the tree grew fair and strong. The storms of ignorance passed over it, and harmed it not. The fierce fires of superstition soared around it; but men leaped into the flames and beat them back, perishing, and the tree grew. With the sweat of their brow have men nourished its green leaves. Their tears have moistened the earth about it. With their blood they have watered its roots.

The seasons have come and passed, and the tree has grown and flourished. And its branches have spread far and high, and ever fresh shoots are bursting forth, and ever new leaves unfolding to the light. But they are all part of the one tree—the tree that was planted on the first birthday of the human race. The stem that bears them springs from the gnarled old trunk that was green and soft when white-haired Time was a little child; the sap that feeds them is drawn up through the roots that twine and twist about the bones of the ages that are dead.

The human mind can no more produce an original thought than a tree can bear an original fruit. As well might one cry for an original note in music as expect an original idea from a human brain.

One wishes our friends, the critics, would grasp this simple truth, and leave off clamoring for the impossible, and being shocked because they do not get it. When a new book is written, the high-class critic opens it with feelings of faint hope, tempered by strong conviction of coming disappointment. As he pores over the pages, his brow darkens with virtuous indignation, and his lip curls with the Godlike contempt that the exceptionally great critic ever feels for everybody in this world, who is not yet dead. Buoyed up by a touching, but totally fallacious, belief that he is performing a public duty, and that the rest of the community is waiting in breathless suspense to learn his opinion of the work in question, before forming any judgment concerning it themselves, he, nevertheless, wearily struggles through about a third of it.

Then his long-suffering soul revolts, and he flings it aside with a cry of despair.

"Why, there is no originality whatever in this," he says. "This book is taken bodily from the Old Testament. It is the story of Adam and Eve all over again. The hero is a mere man! with two arms, two legs, and a head (so called). Why, it is only Moses's Adam under another name! And the heroine is nothing but a woman! and she is described as beautiful, and as having long hair. The author may call her 'Angelina,' or any other name he chooses; but he has evidently, whether he acknowledges it or not, copied her direct from Eve. The characters are barefaced plagiarisms from the book of Genesis! Oh! to find an author with originality!"

One spring I went a walking tour in the country. It was a glorious spring. Not the sort of spring they give us in these miserable times, under this shameless government—a mixture of east wind, blizzard, snow, rain, slush, fog, frost, hail, sleet and thunder-storms—but a sunny, blue-sky'd, joyous spring, such as we used to have regularly every year when I was a young man, and things were different.

It was an exceptionally beautiful spring, even for those golden days; and as I wandered through the waking land, and saw the dawning of the coming green, and watched the blush upon the hawthorn hedge, deepening each day beneath the kisses of the sun, and looked up at the proud old mother trees, dandling their myriad baby buds upon their strong fond arms, holding them high for the soft west wind to caress as he passed laughing by, and marked the primrose yellow creep across the carpet of the woods, and saw the new flush of the field and saw the new light on the hills, and heard the new-found gladness of the birds, and heard from copse and farm and meadow the timid callings of the little new-born things, wondering to find themselves alive, and smelt the freshness of the earth, and felt the promise in the air, and felt a strong hand in the wind, my spirit rose within me. Spring had come to me also, and stirred me with a strange new life, with a strange new hope I, too, was part of nature, and it was spring! Tender leaves and blossoms were unfolding from my heart. Bright flowers of love and gratitude were opening round its roots. I felt new strength in all my limbs. New blood was pulsing through my veins. Nobler thoughts and nobler longings were throbbing through my brain.

As I walked, Nature came and talked beside me, and showed me the world and myself, and the ways of God seemed clearer.

It seemed to me a pity that all the beautiful and precious thoughts and ideas that were crowding in upon me should be lost to my fellow-men, and so I pitched my tent at a little cottage, and set to work to write them down then and there as they came to me.

"It has been complained of me," I said to myself, "that I do not write literary and high class work—at least, not work that is exceptionally literary and high-class. This reproach shall be removed. I will write an article that shall be a classic. I have worked for the ordinary, every-day reader. It is right that I should do something now to improve the literature of my beloved country."

And I wrote a grand essay—though I say it who should not, though I don't see why I shouldn't—all about spring, and the way it made you feel, and what it made you think. It was simply crowded with elevated thoughts and high-class ideas and cultured wit, was that essay. There was only one fault about that essay: it was too brilliant. I wanted commonplace relief. It would have exhausted the average reader; so much cleverness would have wearied him.

I wish I could remember some of the beautiful things in that essay, and here set them down; because then you would be able to see what they were like for yourselves, and that would be so much more simpler than my explaining to you how beautiful they were. Unfortunately, however, I cannot now call to mind any of them.

I was very proud of this essay, and when I got back to town I called on a very superior friend of mine, a critic, and read it to him. I do not care for him to see any of my usual work, because he really is a very superior person indeed, and the perusal of it appears to give him pains inside. But this article, I thought, would do him good.

"What do you think of it?" I asked, when I had finished.

"Splendid," he replied, "excellently arranged. I never knew you were so well acquainted with the works of the old writers. Why, there is scarcely a classic of any note that you have not quoted from. But where—where," he added, musing, "did you get that last idea but two from? It's the only one I don't seem to remember. It isn't a bit of your own, is it?"

He said that, if so, he should advise me to leave it out. Not that it was altogether bad, but that the interpolation of a modern thought among so unique a collection of passages from the ancients seemed to spoil the scheme.

And he enumerated the various dead-and-buried gentlemen from whom he appeared to think I had collated my article.

"But," I replied, when I had recovered my astonishment sufficiently to speak, "it isn't a collection at all. It is all original. I wrote the thoughts down as they came to me. I have never read any of these people you mention, except Shakespeare."

Of course Shakespeare was bound to be among them. I am getting to dislike that man so. He is always being held up before us young authors as a model, and I do hate models. There was a model boy at our school, I remember, Henry Summers; and it was just the same there. It was continually, "Look at Henry Summers! he doesn't put the preposition before the verb, and spell business b-i-z!" or, "Why can't you write like Henry Summers? He doesn't get the ink all over the copy-book and half-way up his back!" We got tired of this everlasting "Look at Henry Summers!" after a while, and so, one afternoon, on the way home, a few of us lured Henry Summers up a dark court; and when he came out again he was not worth looking at.

Now it is perpetually, "Look at Shakespeare!" "Why don't you write like Shakespeare?" "Shakespeare never made that joke. Why don't you joke like Shakespeare?"

If you are in the play-writing line it is still worse for you. "Why don't you write plays like Shakespeare's?" they indignantly say. "Shakespeare never made his comic man a penny steamboat captain." "Shakespeare never made his hero address the girl as 'ducky.' Why don't you copy Shakespeare?" If you do try to copy Shakespeare, they tell you that you must be a fool to attempt to imitate Shakespeare.

Oh, shouldn't I like to get Shakespeare up our street, and punch him!

"I cannot help that," replied my critical friend—to return to our previous question—"the germ of every thought and idea you have got in that article can be traced back to the writers I have named. If you doubt it, I will get down the books, and show you the passages for yourself."

But I declined the offer. I said I would take his word for it, and would rather not see the passages referred to. I felt indignant. "If," as I said, "these men—these Platos and Socrateses and Ciceros and Sophocleses and Aristophaneses and Aristotles and the rest of them had been taking advantage of my absence to go about the world spoiling my business for me, I would rather not hear any more about them."

And I put on my hat and came out, and I have never tried to write anything original since.

I dreamed a dream once. (It is the sort of thing a man would dream. You cannot very well dream anything else, I know. But the phrase sounds poetical and biblical, and so I use it.) I dreamed that I was in a strange country—indeed, one might say an extraordinary country. It was ruled entirely by critics.

The people in this strange land had a very high opinion of critics—nearly as high an opinion of critics as the critics themselves had, but not, of course, quite—that not being practicable—and they had agreed to be guided in all things by the critics. I stayed some years in that land. But it was not a cheerful place to live in, so I dreamed.

There were authors in this country, at first, and they wrote books. But the critics could find nothing original in the books whatever, and said it was a pity that men, who might be usefully employed hoeing potatoes, should waste their time and the time of the critics, which was of still more importance, in stringing together a collection of platitudes, familiar to every school-boy, and dishing up old plots and stories that had already been cooked and recooked for the public until everybody had been surfeited with them.

And the writers read what the critics said and sighed, and gave up writing books, and went off and hoed potatoes; as advised. They had had no experience in hoeing potatoes, and they hoed very badly; and the people whose potatoes they hoed strongly recommended them to leave hoeing potatoes, and to go back and write books. But you can't do what everybody advises.

There were artists also in this strange world, at first, and they painted pictures, which the critics came and looked at through eyeglasses.

"Nothing whatever original in them," said the critics; "same old colors, same old perspective and form, same old sunset, same old sea and land, and sky and figures. Why do these poor men waste their time, painting pictures, when they might be so much more satisfactorily employed on ladders painting houses?"

Nothing, by the by, you may have noticed, troubles your critic more than the idea that the artist is wasting his time. It is the waste of time that vexes the critic; he has such an exalted idea of the value of other people's time. "Dear, dear me!" he says to himself, "why, in the time the man must have taken to paint this picture or to write this book, he might have blacked fifteen thousand pairs of boots, or have carried fifteen thousand hods of mortar up a ladder. This is how the time of the world is lost!"

It never occurs to him that, but for that picture or book, the artist would, in all probability, have been mouching about with a pipe in his mouth, getting into trouble.

It reminds me of the way people used to talk to me when I was a boy. I would be sitting, as good as gold, reading "The Pirate's Lair," when some cultured relative would look over my shoulder and say: "Bah! what are you wasting your time with rubbish for? Why don't you go and do something useful?" and would take the book away from me. Upon which I would get up, and go out to "do something useful;" and would come home an hour afterward, looking like a bit out of a battle picture, having tumbled through the roof of Farmer Bate's greenhouse and killed a cactus, though totally unable to explain how I came to be on the roof of Farmer Bate's greenhouse. They had much better have left me alone, lost in "The Pirate's Lair!"

The artists in this land of which I dreamed left off painting pictures, after hearing what the critics said, and purchased ladders, and went off and painted houses.

Because, you see, this country of which I dreamed was not one of those vulgar, ordinary countries, such as exist in the waking world, where people let the critics talk as much as ever they like, and nobody pays the slightest attention to what they say. Here, in this strange land, the critics were taken seriously, and their advice followed.

As for the poets and sculptors, they were very soon shut up. The idea of any educated person wanting to read modern poetry when he could obtain Homer, or caring to look at any other statue while there was still some of the Venus de Medicis left, was too absurd. Poets and sculptors were only wasting their time.

What new occupation they were recommended to adopt, I forget. Some calling they knew nothing whatever about, and that they were totally unfitted for, of course.

The musicians tried their art for a little while, but they, too, were of no use. "Merely a repetition of the same notes in different combinations," said the critics.

"Why will people waste their time writing unoriginal music, when they might be sweeping crossings?"

One man had written a play. I asked what the critics had said about him. They showed me his tomb.

Then, there being no more artists or *litterateurs* or dramatists or musicians left for their beloved critics to criticise, the general public of this enlightened land said to themselves, "Why should not our critics come and criticise us? Criticism is useful to a man. Have we not often been told so? Look how useful it has been to the artists and writers—saved the poor fellows from wasting their time? Why shouldn't we have some of its benefits?"

They suggested the idea to the critics, and the critics thought it an excellent one, and said they would undertake the job with pleasure. One must say for the critics that they never shirk work. They will sit and criticise for eighteen hours a day, if necessary, or even, if quite unnecessary, for the matter of that. You can't give them too much to criticise. They will criticise everything and everybody in this world. They will criticise everything in the next world, too, when they get there. I expect poor old Pluto has a lively time with them all, as it is.

So, when a man built a house, or a farm-yard hen laid an egg, the critics were asked in to comment on it. They found that none of the houses were original. On every floor were passages that seemed mere copies from passages in other houses. They were all built on the same hackneyed plan; cellars underneath, ground floor level with the street, attic at the top. No originality anywhere!

So, likewise with the eggs. Every egg suggested reminiscences of other eggs.

It was heartrending work.

The critics criticised all things. When a young couple fell in love, they each, before thinking of marriage, called upon the critics for a criticism of the other one.

Needless to say that, in the result, no marriage ever came of it.

"My dear young lady," the critics would say, after the inspection had taken place, "I can discover nothing new whatever about the young man. You would simply be wasting your time in marrying him."

Or, to the young man, it would be:

"Oh, dear, no! Nothing attractive about the girl at all. Who on earth gave you that notion? Simply a lovely face and figure, angelic disposition, beautiful mind, stanch heart, noble character. Why, there must have been nearly a dozen such girls born into the world since its creation. You would be only wasting your time loving her."

They criticised the birds for their hackneyed style of singing, and the flowers for their hackneyed scents and colors. They complained of the weather that it lacked originality—(true, they had not lived out an English spring)—and found fault with the Sun because of the sameness of his methods.

They criticised the babies. When a fresh infant was published in a house, the critics would call in a body to pass their judgment upon it, and the young mother would bring it down for them to sample.

"Did you ever see a child anything like that in this world before?" she would say, holding it out to them. "Isn't it a wonderful baby? *You* never saw a child with legs like that, I know. Nurse says he's the most extraordinary baby she ever attended. Bless him!"

But the critics did not think anything of it.

"Tut, tut," they would reply, "there is nothing extraordinary about that child—no originality whatever. Why, it's exactly like every other baby—bald head, red face, big mouth, and stumpy nose. Why, that's only a weak imitation of the baby next door. It's a plagiarism, that's what that child is. You've been wasting your time, madam. If you can't do anything more original than that, we should advise you to give up the business altogether."

That was the end of criticism in that strange land.

"Oh! look here, we've had enough of you and your originality," said the people to the critics, after that. "Why, *you* are not original, when one comes to think of it, and your criticisms are not original. You've all of you been saying exactly the same thing ever since the time of Solomon. We are going to drown you and have a little peace."

"What, drown a critic!" cried the critics, "never heard of such a monstrous proceeding in our lives!"

"No, we flatter ourselves it is an original idea," replied the public, brutally. "You ought to be charmed with it. Out you come!"

So they took the critics out and drowned them, and then passed a short act, making criticism a capital offense.

After that, the art and literature of the country followed, somewhat, the methods of the quaint and curious school, but the land, notwithstanding, was a much more cheerful place to live in, I dreamed.

But I never finished telling you about the dream in which I thought I left my legs behind me when I went into a certain theater.

I dreamed that the ticket the man gave me for my legs was No. 19, and I was worried all through the performance for fear No. 61 should get hold of them, and leave me his instead. Mine are rather a fine pair of legs, and I am, I confess, a little proud of them—at all events, I prefer them to anybody else's. Besides, number sixty-one's might be a skinny pair, and not fit me.

It quite spoiled my evening, fretting about this.

Another extraordinary dream I had was one in which I dreamed that I was engaged to be married to my Aunt Jane. That was not, however, the extraordinary part of it; I have often known people to dream things like that. I knew a man who once dreamed that he was actually married to his own mother-in-law! He told me that never in his life had he loved the alarm clock with more deep and grateful tenderness than he did that morning. The dream almost reconciled him to being married to his real wife. They lived quite happily together for a few days, after that dream.

No; the extraordinary part of my dream was, that I knew it was a dream. "What on earth will uncle say to this engagement?" I thought to myself, in my dream. "There's bound to be a row about it. We shall have a deal of trouble with uncle, I feel sure." And this thought quite troubled me until the sweet reflection came: "Ah! well, it's only a dream."

And I made up my mind that I would wake up as soon as uncle found out about the engagement, and leave him and Aunt Jane to fight the matter out between themselves.

It is a very great comfort, when the dream grows troubled and alarming, to feel that it is only a dream, and to know that we shall awake soon and be none the worse for it. We can dream out the foolish perplexity with a smile then.

Sometimes the dream of life grows strangely troubled and perplexing, and then he who meets dismay the bravest is he who feels that the fretful play is but a dream—a brief, uneasy dream of three score years and ten, or thereabouts, from which, in a little while, he will awake—at least, he dreams so.

How dull, how impossible life would be without dreams—waking dreams, I mean—the dreams that we call "castles in the air," built by the kindly hands of Hope! Were it not for the mirage of the oasis, drawing his footsteps ever onward, the weary traveler would lie down in the desert sand and die. It is the mirage of distant success, of happiness that, like the bunch of carrots fastened an inch beyond the donkey's nose, seems always just within our reach, if only we will gallop fast enough, that makes us run so eagerly along the road of Life.

Providence, like a father with a tired child, lures us ever along the way with tales and promises, until, at the frowning gate that ends the road, we shrink back, frightened. Then, promises still more sweet he stoops and whispers in our ear, and timid yet partly reassured, and trying to hide our fears, we gather up all that is left of our little stock of hope and, trusting yet half afraid, push out our groping feet into the darkness.